O9-CFU-131

Tiffky Doofky

· WILLIAM STEIG ·

A Sunburst Book

Michael di Capua Books

Farrar, Straus and Giroux

E
Steig

Jonathan 2005

To Delia, Sidonie, Nika,
Abigail, Sylvain, and Estelle

Copyright © 1978 by William Steig
All rights reserved
Library of Congress catalog card number: 78-19657
Published in Canada by Collins Publishers, Toronto
Printed in Singapore
First edition, 1978
Sunburst edition, 1987

Tiffky Doofky, the garbage collector, went his rounds in a jolly mood. It was first-rate weather. He planned to wind up work in time to get to the Annual Picnic of the Oil & Vinegar Club over in Moose Hollow.

He had already collected a truckload of stuff: muck, slops, dirt, rags, cinders, corncobs, bones, bottles, cans, paper, fur and feathers from the barbershop, all sorts of junk and gimcracks, and the rubbish from the carnival that had just come to town.

At Madam Tarsal's place, adding her trash to his truck, he made up his mind to get his fortune told. On such a day, something out of the ordinary was bound to happen, and he had to know what it was going to be.

Madam Tarsal led him behind a curtain, where an amber light shone on a round table. Tiffky sat with his mouth open as she peered into the crystal ball. Suddenly her little eyes lit up. "My dear Tiffky Doofky," she quacked, "guess what I see in the crystal ball! This very day, before the sun goes down, you will fall in love with the one you are going to marry. Nothing you do can keep it from happening."

Tiffky Doofky's tail whacked the chair he was sitting on. "Is it anyone I already know?" he asked.

"It is no one you know," said the fortuneteller, dropping her lids.

Tiffky Doofky hoisted his suspenders, kissed Madam Tarsal smack on the beak, sailed out to his truck, and headed for the town dump. He was already dreaming of his love-to-be; she put him in mind of rosebuds, dew-drops, starlight, chocolate pudding. The stink of the garbage did not faze him. He respected garbage. The furniture in his home, the bed he slept

on, the dishes he ate from, his footstool, his lamp, his umbrella, the pictures on his walls, all came out of the garbage. The clothes he wore came out of the garbage—a patch here, a stitch there, and he was even a bit of a dude, with arm garters, and spats in season.

"Maybe I'll find her at the dump," he mused as he barreled along. "But more likely it'll be at the Oil & Vinegar Club picnic."

Soon the dump lay before him, a sea of garbage. Crows were rummaging in the debris for dainty tidbits.

Tiffky tilted the bin of his truck. As the slops slid and tumbled out, something caught his quick eye: a necklace agleam with emeralds on a bed of sauerkraut. He lifted it with careful paws. How lovely! He would have to find out who had lost it. Meanwhile, he fastened it around his own neck.

His day's work done, he was ready now for the picnic. He put his truck in reverse, backed up, wheeled around, and rattled down Nocknagel Road. Near Wottle Corners he caught up with a chicken pedaling a bike. He honked and prepared to pass, but the bike curved and keeled over and the chicken lay under it, kicking and clucking.

Tiffky hit the brake and leaped out. "Darn these newfangled bikes!" the chicken ranted. She was an old biddy with a red babushka. "Whisked me around like a whirligig!" she went on. "Something amiss with those wacky wheels."

"Are you okay, ma'am?" asked Tiffky Doofky.

"Don't know yet," said the biddy. "Help me up, young fellow, don't just stand there like a totem pole!" Tiffky got her under the wings and heaved her up to her feet. She shook, blinked, shifted her shawl. "I'm back in shape," she announced. "Much obliged."

"Then I'll be trotting along," Tiffky said. "Going to meet my love today, before the sun goes down."

"I know," said the biddy, "and that's her necklace you're wearing." Tiffky looked at the old chicken in astonishment. He was always ready to believe in magic. "You've done me a favor, young fellow," declared the biddy. "I'm going to do you a favor. One good turn merits another. Correct?" Tiffky wished she'd hurry up. It was getting late, as he could see by the watch he'd found at the dump last Christmas.

The old biddy took a small bow and arrow out of her basket. Lifting her skirt, she pulled three feathers from her left thigh. She pressed the feathers to her beak, mumbling mysterious words, and swiftly fletched the arrow with the feathers. "Young fellow," she said, "I will shoot this magic arrow with this magic bow. Follow whither it leads and there you will find your true love."

"I appreciate this," said Tiffky.

"Tut, tut," clucked the old biddy, "it's just a trifle. Nothing to get flustered over. Enjoy what follows." She squinted one of her red-rimmed eyes, aimed the arrow, and let it zing.

"Thanks again!" yelled Tiffky, and he was off with the arrow, racing down the road.

(The old biddy was really a villainous witch who detested Madam Tarsal, her fellow fowl, and always tried to foil her fortunetelling. As Tiffky Doofky ran after the arrow, she cackled with evil glee.)

After going straight for a while, the arrow swerved left. Then it switched and swooped right, then it described some crazy circles and zipped off in a new direction, with Tiffky keeping apace of it. All at once it dipsy-doodled, looped off left again, zigging and zagging around trees and out into a field, where it fell to the ground.

There stood a lady, slender and graceful, holding a parasol. Tiffky's heart hammered as he approached her, his cap in his paw. He was not worried about what he would say; the right words always came when he needed them.

Grinning, he bowed, with his tail in a strong curve. When he straightened up to look into her eyes, there were no eyes to look into. There was no face! Only a shock of straw. The lady was a scarecrow!

How unpleasant! Tiffky Doofky started back to his truck. But when he got where he thought he was going, there was no sign of the truck. Or of the road he had left it on.

He walked this way, then that way. It was not the same world as before. Where was he? He walked further, looking for something familiar, trying to get his bearings.

A well-dressed cat, perched on a tree stump, was strumming a mandolin with his claws, perfectly at home in this strange place. Tiffky went over to him, feeling shy. "Sir? Excuse me," he said, "have you seen a garbage truck?"

"Garbage truck? What's that?" queried the cat. He had lazy yellow eyes.

"Are we anywhere near Nocknagel Road, town of Popville?"

"Never heard of either," said the cat.

"Then I'm loster than I thought I was," said Tiffky.

"Perhaps I can help," the cat suggested, laying down his mandolin.

"I was on my way to a picnic. I'm supposed to be meeting my future wife today, before the sun goes down."

"H'm," said the cat, stroking a whisker, "the sun is pretty low already. Let me have a button off your vest, will you?" And without waiting for leave to do so, he took out a pocket scissors and snipped a button from Tiffky's vest. Holding the button between his paws, he closed his yellow eyes and recited:

> *I ask this button off his vest,*
> *Should he go east or should he go west?*
> *Should he go north or should he go south?*
> *Put the answer in my mouth.*

He waited a few moments, then, "Oom, ba-ba-loom," he said, "your truck is on the far side of that ridge."

"Sir, many thanks," said Tiffky, and he hurried off. On the far side of the ridge he heard sweet bells dingling, but saw no bells. He heard a voice calling, "*Ti-i-iffky Doo-oo-oofky. Ti-i-iffky Doo-oo-oofky.*" But he saw no one. He was no coward, but he began to feel uneasy. "This way, Tiffky," said the voice. He walked toward it, listening, and then: there . . . was . . . no . . . ground . . . beneath . . . his . . . feet . . . He was falling, falling and turning, turning and falling, and thud! he met the ground and lay there in a stupor. The hazy world wobbled round him.

Some cows ambled by, nodding, chewing, and mooing.

Tiffky lay there a long time. When he opened his eyes, he could see the cliff he had fallen over. He ached. He knew it was very late. How could he possibly get to the picnic, he wondered, and meet his love? Well, hadn't Madam Tarsal said nothing could keep him from meeting her? Why worry and get wrinkles? It would happen.

A man with a net darted past, chasing a butterfly. He raced back to where Tiffky lay and stood over him, staring, but saying nothing.

"I fell over that cliff," explained Tiffky.

"I know," said the man. "I've been waiting for you to come to. I wanted to ask you, are there any butterflies up there?" Unexpectedly, he put the net over his head and turned a somersault.

"I didn't see any," said Tiffky, getting up. "Tiffky Doofky's the name. Who are you?"

"Me? I'm a lunatic," said the butterfly hunter.

"Oh," said Tiffky. "Then probably you wouldn't know the way to Nocknagel Road."

"Oh yes, I would," the lunatic asserted. "Nocknagel Road is right down th——" And he *vanished* before Tiffky's astounded eyes. The cliff, the whole scene, melted and was gone, and Tiffky was back on Nocknagel Road! (How the devil did this happen? Well, the old biddy who had

been holding him under a spell had to go home in order to lay an egg. This egg demanded all her attention, and tired her. So she turned herself into a pair of old sneakers, something she did now and then because she found it restful. Tiffky Doofky had been forgotten, he was off the hook.)

He flopped down on a rock, exhausted. The sun was low and in flames. Well, Madam Tarsal had better get a new crystal ball. The day was about done and no civilized soul to fall in love with was anywhere to be seen. Only swallows swooping after insects.

Tiffky Doofky nodded. At the third and deepest nod, the world went away and he was asleep. A dream came: Madam Tarsal flew overhead, her crystal ball clutched in her webbed feet. As she passed over him, he found himself face to face with his love. They were sitting in a field of daisies, caressing one another. Her embrace was gentle, sinuous. But it began getting stronger. And stronger. And suddenly . . .

Tiffky Doofky jumped to his feet. He was wide awake and in the coils of a boa constrictor! He tugged at the powerful snake, but it only tightened its hold. "Help!" he shouted. "Help!" But soon he could shout no longer. The breath of life was being pressed out of him. He decided to face death with dignity. The sun was now on the rim of the earth, about to leave this gruesome scene. "Goodbye, dear world," said Tiffky in his mind. "Goodbye, great sun. And goodbye, love, whoever, wherever you are!"

Someone came tearing down the road. "Dolores!" she shouted. "At ease!" The boa constrictor instantly loosened its hold, then carefully unwound itself from around Tiffky Doofky and lay obediently on the ground. It had escaped from its coop at the carnival. Tiffky's rescuer was Estrella, the snake's fearless trainer.

Tiffky had never seen anyone who looked so good to him. It took him no time at all to fall in love. "That's my necklace you're wearing!" said Estrella. "Where on earth did you find it?"

"At the dump when I was ungoading the larbage today," Tiffky heard himself say. His mind had stopped working. He was entranced.

"You're a garbage collector! My dear father was a garbage collector! What a coincidence!" Estrella was sure she had never met anyone so manly yet modest as the one who stood before her, dazed with love.

They gazed at each other with eyes brimful of feeling. As the sun sank below the horizon, both were bathed in the same golden afterglow.

Madam Tarsal knew her onions after all!